The Last Freedom

PRAISE FOR *STORYSHARES*

"One of the brightest innovators and game-changers in the education industry."
– Forbes

"Your success in applying research-validated practices to promote literacy serves as a valuable model for other organizations seeking to create evidence-based literacy programs."

- Library of Congress

"We need powerful social and educational innovation, and Storyshares is breaking new ground. The organization addresses critical problems facing our students and teachers. I am excited about the strategies it brings to the collective work of making sure every student has an equal chance in life."
– Teach For America

"Around the world, this is one of the up-and-coming trailblazers changing the landscape of literacy and education."
- International Literacy Association

"It's the perfect idea. There's really nothing like this. I mean wow, this will be a wonderful experience for young people."   - Andrea Davis Pinkney, Executive Director, Scholastic

"Reading for meaning opens opportunities for a lifetime of learning. Providing emerging readers with engaging texts that are designed to offer both challenges and support for each individual will improve their lives for years to come. Storyshares is a wonderful start."
- David Rose, Co-founder of CAST & UDL

The Last Freedom

Kenzi Melody

STORYSHARES

Story Share, Inc.
New York. Boston. Philadelphia.

Storyshares
Story Share, Inc.
24 N. Bryn Mawr Avenue #340
Bryn Mawr, PA 19010-3304
www.storyshares.org

Inspiring reading with a new kind of book.

Interest Level: High School
Grade Level Equivalent: 3.1

9781642611960

Book design by Storyshares

Printed in the United States of America

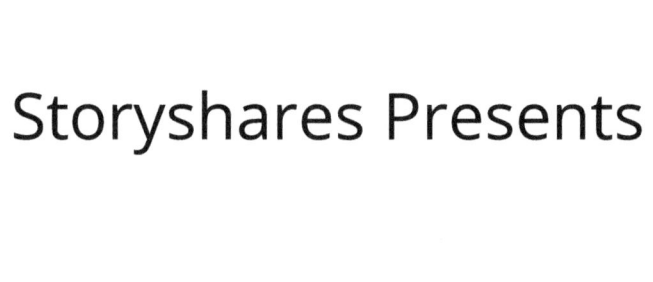

Storyshares Presents

1

She was different.

Different was bad.

Hundreds of years ago, the elders of our city made everyone the same: black hair, gray eyes. Sameness meant less fighting. Less fighting meant peace, and peace was everything. My parents had told me ancient stories of the days when humans struggled with weaknesses, like sickness or pain.

We didn't.

She did.

No one knew where she came from. One day she walked through the gates of our city and stayed. She called herself Eve. Of course we were suspicious of her. Her hair was red, and her eyes were brown. Not even in my wildest imaginations had I pictured such a thing, though I knew it had been common long ago.

Eve was weak.

She got sick, she bled, and she felt pain, but she didn't seem to mind. In fact, when people mentioned her inadequacies, she just laughed. Once, she told me that the things we saw as weak were really what made her strong. I didn't understand, but it made me curious.

I was one of Eve's only friends. They told me not to go near her—her weakness might rub off on me, but I wasn't worried. I had been born a Strong One. There was nothing even she could do to change that.

After a while, even Eve's strangeness became a normal part of the city. The gossip about where she came from was as common as bartering in the marketplace. Eventually, the beacon of her red hair melted seamlessly into the waves of raven-colored sameness surrounding it. Peace had been restored.

And peace was everything.

But one day, one more, and all at once, the peace deserted us.

The Last Freedom

2

It was the forest.

All my life, I'd been warned about it. It hovered on the horizon just out of reach of the city walls, like an army waiting to attack. Once, I asked my parents why we feared it. They didn't know. They'd simply been told by their parents that we should.

Eve had more questions. She wouldn't let it go. It was almost like an obsession. She needed to know what lived there, if anything had ever come out of it, and how we knew it was to be feared. I pretended like I knew the answers to her questions, but I could tell she saw through my lies.

Then she asked if anyone had ever gone into it.

"Of course not," I replied, even though I had no idea. "Why would they?"

"Well, to see what's in there, of course. To see if it's really anything to be afraid of."

"It is something to be afraid of."

"You don't know that."

"Yes, I do. They told me."

"But you don't know for sure. You've never been there."

"I don't need to have been there. Dark things live in the forest."

"But hasn't anyone ever been brave enough to go see if those tales are true?"

"Hasn't anyone ever been what enough?" I asked.

She cocked her head and gave me a funny look. "Brave enough. I said brave enough."

I wrinkled my nose. "That's one of your made-up words, isn't it?"

"I don't make up words."

"Yes, you do. I've never heard that one before."

Eve sighed. "No, of course you haven't."

A few weeks later, something came out of the forest. One of the guards above the gates noticed it first. He told the elders. Soon everyone in the city was crowded atop the walls, watching as an old woman in a tattered white robe emerged from the trees. She shuffled across the open space toward the gate, never looking up and never slowing down.

I began to feel fear creeping over the crowds as the woman approached. There was no way for her to enter the walled city unless we allowed it, but still . . . nothing had ever come out of the forest before. I had been told terribly dark stories about the forest. It seemed natural to be afraid.

One by one, the mothers began dragging the children away from the walls. The crowd thinned until mostly the men and a few older teenagers were left. I started to leave but stayed when I saw Eve standing straight as an arrow, staring out into the field. If someone as weak as she could stand there without fear, surely I could as well. I edged closer to her.

Every step sent jolts of electricity through my veins. I didn't know why the woman frightened me.

At last, one of the elders demanded the woman tell us her business.

She stopped below the gates and looked up, her withered voice sailing on the wind. "I have come to propose a trade. Give me the soul of one of your people, and I shall give you the one freedom you lack."

The elder scoffed, though something in his eyes didn't agree with his tone. "We are already free from pain, strife, and illness. We need nothing else."

"Ah," the old woman laughed, "but the greatest enemy yet remains. While it stalks your streets, all other freedoms are useless."

"A soul is not worth that cost."

"You know in your heart it is. Your people are imprisoned."

"You're wasting your time. Who will go?" The elders were shaking. I could see sweat glistening on the brow of the one who spoke. Clearly they understood something I did not. How could any freedom be worth the cost of a life? We were already free. Despite the walls surrounding us, we had everything we needed.

"I will go."

3

The words were so soft, at first I thought they may have been the cry of a child. But when I saw the look on Eve's face, I knew it was she who had spoken.

I stared at her. "You can't be serious."

She turned to me. "Of course I am. The freedom she offers is the greatest there is."

"How can you know that?"

"Because I have it."

"But your soul!"

"It'll be alright."

The elders didn't try to stop Eve from leaving the city. No one did. Perhaps they were glad she would be gone, that her strange life would be sacrificed in order to add one more freedom to their repertoire.

I ran the length of the wall to where I had the best view of what was happening below. The woman stood still as the gates opened and Eve came toward her. The gates clanged shut. Eve took a step closer. The woman reached out and put a hand on her throat. Eve's skin glowed.

For a moment there was silence. Then a great rumbling noise rolled down from the sky. A tremor snaked through the wall. I was seized by a sensation I'd never felt in my life, something so unbearable that it seemed to be squeezing my heart with an enormous fist. Was this pain?

The others seemed to feel it, too. All at once the walls began to empty as we poured down into the city, crying for help, but there was no help there. The rumbling continued. Something crashed to my left. Billowing dust choked my lungs. I fell face down in the street, gasping for breath.

Slowly the air began to clear.

The pain stopped. I pushed myself onto my knees and looked around.

Light poured down into the streets of the city, running between the cobblestones like liquid gold. The air was warmer than I remembered. I realized with a start that I could see the sky in front of me. The edge of the world hung like an emerald just within reach.

The walls were gone.

After that, the city was different. People fought with one another. Children stayed out too long in the cold and came back coughing. Sometimes my head or my stomach would be so full of pain, I couldn't stand up.

But there was light in the streets every day. People laughed. Singing echoed from front doors in the morning. When we looked back on it in years to come, we found that no one missed the walls. The woman had been right—there is no freedom in the world greater than freedom from fear.

I've often wondered since that day how a Weak One could have changed everything.

She gave us pain.

She gave us sickness.

She took our peace.

In its place, she gave us laughter. She made us curious. She showed us hope.

She was different.

Now we all are.

About The Author

Kenzi Melody is a contributing author to the Storyshares library.

About The Publisher

Story Shares is a nonprofit focused on supporting the millions of teens and adults who struggle with reading by creating a new shelf in the library specifically for them. The ever-growing collection features content that is compelling and culturally relevant for teens and adults, yet still readable at a range of lower reading levels.

Story Shares generates content by engaging deeply with writers, bringing together a community to create this new kind of book. With more intriguing and approachable stories to choose from, the teens and adults who have fallen behind are improving their skills and beginning to discover the joy of reading. For more information, visit storyshares.org.

Easy to Read. Hard to Put Down.

www.ingramcontent.com/pod-product-compliance
Lightning Source LLC
Chambersburg PA
CBHW071231170626
46809CB00005BA/2035